Aeison

# THE
# FROZEN DOZEN

familiar Stories?

Acy

# THE
# FROZEN DOZEN

Alexander Flint

Rutledge Books Inc.  Danbury, Connecticut

ALL RIGHTS RESERVED
Rutledge Books, Inc.
107 Mill Plain Road, Danbury, CT 06811
1-800-278-8533
www.rutledgebooks.com

Manufactured in the United States of America

**Cataloging in Publication Data**
Flint, Alexander
   The Frozen Dozen

   ISBN: 1-58244-229-0

   1. Fiction

Library of Congress Control Number: 2002112954

# Contents

# The Ballroom Dancer

Elizabeth Longsworth Pennington of the Scarsdale Longsworths was seated at her dining table for four in the prestigious Queen's Grill. World-cruise passengers were always lodged on the sun deck, the most expensive residence area available in the cruise packages. The five-hundred-thousand-dollar price of the fifteen-week vacation allowed them the privilege of being berthed in the Grand Suite, which came with butler service, room service, a freshly stocked mini-bar, a refrigerator, fresh fruit, and personalized stationery.

Elizabeth's favorite time of the day was dinnertime in the Queen's Grill. Each of the forty dinner guests had no less than two waitpersons, as well as a wine steward. Elizabeth enjoyed giving orders. More often than not she would send her dinner back to be reheated even though it was sufficiently hot. She thrived on hearing apologies from servants. It made her feel so powerful. It was the twenty-ninth day since their departure from New York on 6 January. It was a formal night; evening wear was required for dinner and in all public areas. Elizabeth had seventy-six different formal outfits. Harold had tried to talk her out of bringing so much opulence due to the logistical difficulty, but she would not be swayed. Elizabeth had waited thirty years for Harold to retire, and now she would flaunt her success.

At 7:10 PM Elizabeth became furious when Harold slowly leaned forward and gently placed his face into his soup. It was a succulent mix of beef broth with calf's-liver dumplings. Harold had always loved calf's liver dumplings, but showing his appreciation this way was going too far. Sometimes Harold was a great kidder, but this was really too much. Elizabeth was so angry she actually screamed, "Harold!"

In the past when she disapproved of his alcohol-induced behavior Elizabeth had simply had to raise an eyebrow. Now Harold's reaction was to blow bubbles into the soup through his nose. She became enraged seeing the way he made the dumplings dance around with his nasal turbulence. How did he do that, she wondered? Harold always amazed Elizabeth by displaying skills she never knew he had. She was ready to forgive him when he stopped for a moment and raised his head to look at her, but then, with what seemed like a slight smile, he immersed his face back in the soup and resumed his vulgar antics. Didn't he realize he was humiliating her? "The bastard," she thought. Well, she would not remain here amid this majestic regalia and have it appear as if she accepted his unruly behavior. Elizabeth got up and stormed out of the Queen's Grill which was located on the boat deck, the most prestigious of five QE 2 restaurants.

Marek, the table captain, immediately recognized that the man was in physical distress. He sent the waiter, Armand, to call for medical assistance and summon the dining room manager. Within a few short minutes Harold Pennington, a financial advisor to the greatest leaders in the world was in a wheelchair on his way the doctor's office on deck 2 by stairway G.

The dining went on as usual in the Queen's Grill. Wine was uncorked, and the second course of farfal alle zucchini (pasta with zucchini, basil, mint garlic, and pecorino cheese) was being wheeled in. Meanwhile, in the kitchen the main courses—grilled sea bass fillet coated with lemon pepper on squid risotto with red wine butter sauce, turkey schnitzel Parisienne with cucumber potato salad, veal Cordon Bleu (breaded scallop of veal filled with Swiss cheese and ham), and chateaubriand with chive hollandaise and Lyonnaise potatoes—were waiting to be served. The "sweet indulgences," a euphemism for desserts—chocolate marquise, kumquat confit, warm peach tart with cinnamon parfait, and hot hazelnut soufflé—had been portioned out earlier and were queued up, each awaiting its turn on the great Queen's Grill stage.

By the time the salad (on this night it was a jalapeno Caesar with crisp chorizo) followed the fateful soup, none of the restaurant patrons were discussing the medical emergency that had occurred during the previous course. The incident was completely forgotten.

Elizabeth, who was in her cabin, was still seething with anger. Harold had humiliated her once too often, and on a formal night, too. She decided to attend the ball in the Grand Lounge and make use of the numerous gentlemen hosts provided by the ship's crew as dancing partners for single ladies.

When the doctor ascertained that Harold was indeed dead he stepped out into his waiting room to inform the wife of the deceased. Dr. Granger was surprised to find that his waiting room was empty. He went to the deceased's cabin and knocked softly. When his knock was not answered he entered the lavish suite with his master key and found it empty. He then informed Master Captain Wright of his dilemma. The officer immediately instituted a search of the ship so the newly widowed Mrs. Pennington could be notified of the sad news.

Elizabeth Longsworth Pennington was dancing in the Grand Ballroom when she saw the ship's captain approaching. A new wave of anger swept over her as she was reminded of her husband acting like such an ass. She wondered what additional humiliating news she would be given now, and by the ship's captain, no less.

"Mrs. Pennington, may I have a word with you privately, please?" Captain Wright said gently.

"Shit," Elizabeth thought. "What did that moron do now?"

"Madam, I have some sad news for you," he said when they were in the hall next to the closed Tour and Travel office.

This time Elizabeth thought, "Double shit, he must have really created a scene when I left." She felt she had made the right move by leaving immediately, at the beginning of his untoward behavior.

"Madam, I regret to inform you that your husband is dead," said the captain. Captin Wright observed that surprised, look accompanied by wide eyes and a slight smile crossed the face of Mrs. Pennington. "My God," he thought. "It appears to be a look of relief."

Upon hearing the news, Elizabeth who was expecting to have to apologize again for her husband's behavior, was actually quite relieved.

"I am so sorry, Captain," she began. "He is always doing that, you know."

"Dying?" the surprised captain replied.

"Why, no, I meant causing a disturbance," Elizabeth said.

Captain Wright rubbed the whitish beard on his chin, and with a puzzled voice, asked, "Would you like to come to my cabin where I will call the chaplain for grief counseling, madam?"

"No, Captain," she heard herself say. "I would rather dance in the ballroom." She glided off toward the sounds of Glenn Miller's "In the Mood."

# THE BURLESQUE QUEEN

The Island of St. Helena was the exile site of Napoleon. From 1815 until his death in 1821, the former French emperor enjoyed the beauty of this volcanic island. It is located 1,150 miles off the west coast of Africa at 16( south latitude and 5( 45' west longitude. The area of the island is 47 square miles. It is about 10 miles long and 6 miles wide at its extreme points. Marine erosion has formed majestic perpendicular cliffs that rise from 450 to 2,000 feet high on the east, north, and west coasts. The only practical landing site is James Bay, which is located on the leeward side of the island.

The government of St. Helena is administered by a governor. The St. Helena Royal Instructions provide for an executive council consisting of the government secretary and the colonial treasurer. There are also several members of an advisory council. The governor appoints everyone in the government. There is a Supreme Court with a chief justice, the only judge, who is also the governor.

Sir James Cheshire, the governor, ruled his island with an iron fist. Codes and regulations were innumerable and entangling. Sir James liked it that way. It gave him more power. Anything to do with the government took weeks. If by chance a tourist should have a legal dispute to be settled, he would be retained on the island until the matter was settled in the courts, or, like Napoleon, until his death. A death on the island constituted a major problem.

Frank Passalaqua had made two major mistakes in his seventy-five years of life. His first was marrying Angie Riccobono, and his last occurred while visiting St. Helena with her. He'd had to listen to Angie's constant complaints for the last forty years, but her whining on this cruise was intolerable. She constantly belittled Frank, chiding him about the number of hot dogs he ate. She was only quiet when losing money at the casino.

Angie had been a great dancer in her youth, but her talents, the least of which were intellectual, ended there. She was now overweight, and dumber. It was not that advancing years had slowed Angie's intelligence. She had never been intelligent in the first place. On two separate occasions Angie had been severely burned by holding a Roman candle upside-down on New Dorp Beach during fourth of July celebrations. Instead of the fireball shooting upward toward the sky, it had exploded with its fury against her chest. She had suffered painful burns. Most people learn from their mistakes. Angie was not like most people. The second time Angie held the Roman candle upside-down, she had extended her arm to a greater length, turned her head to the side, and closed her eyes. She had been burned again. There was no third occasion; she refused to partake in further pyrotechnic celebrations.

Frank and Angie Passalaqua were on the vacation of their life. Frank had retired from his restaurant business of forty years and they were going to enjoy their trip around the world. They had met in a romantic manner. Angie had been a burlesque dancer at the old Hudson Theater in Hudson, New Jersey, in the 1950s. Her body was her greatest attribute. Frank sold hot dogs outside the entrance to theater patrons. Frank always gave the theater manager free franks in return for being allowed to stand in the rear of the theater and watch the strippers. Eventually Frank was able to use the girls' hunger as a way to meet them.

Angie Riccobono had liked Frank from the first moment she had met him; he always had a roll of bills in his pocket and a hot dog with plenty of mustard in his hand. She was quite impressed with him. Her influence on Frank encouraged him to trade his hot-dog pushcart for a wagon which he attached to the back of a 1949 Mercury, and he moved his business to Hylan Boulevard on Staten Island, in NY, where he sold and ate his hot dogs for the next forty years.

Angie told the friends she had made in the gambling casino, located portside on the QE 2, that they had retired after they had sold their posh (she used the word posh) New York City restaurant. She had never mentioned that it was a wagon on the side of a highway, which in later years had become a van.

On the beautiful sunny day of 5 April 2000, Angie immediately began complaining when she realized that she was not on the island of Monaco. She somehow had been under the mistaken assumption that she was going ashore to visit the casinos of Prince Rainier. She had always loved Grace Kelly and hoped that maybe she would see her. Angie had no concept of geography, either. When the ship had berthed at Durban, South Africa, she had asked if she could visit the pyramids. She had asked the same question in Sydney, Australia. Angie had again displayed a certain diminished mental capacity while on a tour of Sydney when she indicated her disappointment in seeing no kangaroos hopping around the city.

Frank Passalaqua died while on a two-hour bus tour of the island of St. Helena. A passenger across the aisle saw him move his eyeglasses upward to rest on his forehead and squeeze the bridge of his nose with his thumb and forefinger. Frank held a pose with his head back against the seat and his eyeglasses resting on his forehead for about twenty minutes. It was the usual signal he gave when he was annoyed with his wife's complaining. The passengers were alerted that something was amiss when Angie loudly complained that her jerk of a husband could sleep and fart anywhere. "It's no wonder he fell asleep," she complained. "After missing breakfast he gulps down four hot dogs at the pier. What do you expect?"

Because a passenger of the QE 2 had died on Sir James' island, the entire ship, its 2,500 passengers, and its crew were likely to be held on the island. All deaths had to be investigated by the proper authorities, and Sir James Cheshire would have to approve the ship's release. This meant that weeks might pass before Sir James was satisfied that the paperwork was in order.

The ship, its passengers, and its crew had a hero they would never forget. Kathleen Reilly, a good citizen of County Cork and a member of the purser's staff, had the good sense to call the ship on her cell phone. She was assigned to the tour in the event of just such an emergency. Her instructions were to return to the ship with everyone on the bus and make no stops.

Dr. Michael Goodwin, a Welsh physician who had boarded at Port Elizabeth, South Africa, realized Mr. Passalaqua was, indeed, quite dead. He told Angie that he believed her husband's death had been instantaneous, probably caused by a massive myocardial infarct.

"A what?" Angie asked.

"A massive myocardial infarct," the physician repeated.

"An internal fart! I knew those hot dogs would kill him."

At portside Jamestown, a wheelchair was waiting along with the ship's doctor. In his old-fashioned black leather doctor's bag were some unusual, nonmedicinal items to be used for transporting Frank back to the ship. On the bus, out of sight of the immigration authorities, Frank was taped into the wheelchair, which had to be partially folded to fit through the bus doors. The body was covered with two blankets to hide the silver duct tape. From the black doctor's bag also came a pair of oversized, extra-dark sunglasses. The duct tape was passed around the chest of the corpse, around the biceps, forearms, thighs, and calves, securing it to the wheelchair. A wire hoop was formed to wrap under the armpits and pass under the shirt and was shaped into an oval to support Frank's chin, holding his head in place. The final touch was a scarf placed around his neck to hide the wire head support.

Angie was detained on the bus while members of the ship's staff chatted with Frank as they wheeled him past the customs and immigration authorities. Sir James was none the wiser. Angie was oblivious, too, to all of the unusual activity taking place on the bus. When asked by Kathleen Reilly how she was holding up, she asked, "Are there any kangaroos here?"

# THE COP

John Ryan was a retired New York City police sergeant. He had spent twenty-five years on the job in the toughest city in the world. The job was not tough in the sense of having to deal with the worst or the most criminals, but it got tough when the cop had to deal with the bureaucracy of his own department. The bullet-proof vest he'd had to wear in recent years was ample protection against a bullet striking the torso; there were many stories of cops surviving shoot-outs in which the bad guys were dropped. But the vest did not protect against a head shot, nor did it protect against the shotgun-like shrapnel constantly fired at him from the bosses within his own ranks. John Ryan hated his bosses as much as he hated the street scum. He felt surrounded by both.

Sergeant Ryan was more at ease when he was on the dirty streets of his precinct, more so than when he was at home with his dull wife of twenty-six years. He loved the power that came from his presence. Ryan considered anyone who was not a cop a bad guy. When he spoke to the inhabitants of his precinct, he oozed contempt for them. When he spoke to anyone at all, his attitude was one of hate laced with sarcasm.

His arrogance was often transmitted to his fellow cops, his family, and his friends. John Ryan did not have many friends. The only socializing he did was at Steve's Pub, the neighborhood bar he frequented after work. He led all discussions, and his opinion was expected to be received as gospel. The one thing Ryan liked most, whether on the street, in the pub, or at home, was to be dominant.

Sergeant Ryan experienced the greatest sense of power when he apprehended a criminal. He would loudly belittle the criminal until he felt a sense of pride swelling within him. Ryan enjoyed the moments before he was actually committed to making the arrest. He liked to see the defeated, begging look in the eyes of his quarry. He treated his collars like prey, like a cat toying with a sad, crippled bird before the kill. Ryan was constantly given new partners because very few cops could stand being around him. If his collar could offer something valuable in return, there would be no arrest. He would accept the names of drug suppliers, information relating to a more serious crime about to occur, or the whereabouts of a fugitive. The offering he wanted most of all, and frequently received, was the use of the criminal's wife or girlfriend. He got to enjoy sex with women when they were frightened and helpless. The poor woman feared a beating from the cop, or from the boyfriend/husband, if she didn't please Ryan. Sergeant Ryan was often able to find out how the woman felt if she lost her man to prison. If the loss was severe, he would use that knowledge in future encounters with the hapless woman.

None of his abnormal sex worked with his wife, Mary Ryan. She would have none of his sadistic sex games when he had first tried them on her. She tongue-lashed him and lectured him about what the sisters had taught her at St. Agatha's School in Bay Ridge, Brooklyn. Mary had been taught that sex was for procreation and not for fun.

For some reason, the good Lord had intervened and had prevented conception. Mary assumed He thought John was too immature. Maybe next year John will become worthier, she thought. But John never became deserving, and he never matured. The Ryan family was to remain at two.

John didn't care that he wasn't a father. This way, remaining childless, Mary would continue working, and the financial resources of the family would remain secure. John would not have to hustle with second jobs like his two New York City firefighter brothers. Sean and Tim always had to take additional jobs to assure the financial and educational security of their massive brood of noisy, runny-nosed children. No, John Ryan didn't mind the absence of parenthood at all.

When John finally retired after twenty-five years, he thought he could continue his life, going to Steve's Pub, following the local sports teams, and being more knowledgeable in worldly matters that the other drunks around him. He was surprised when Mary announced that they were going to take a three-month cruise around the world on the QE 2.

"What's a QE 2?" he demanded.

"It's a luxury cruise ship, you moron," Mary replied. "We leave January sixth from New York, sail around the frigging world, and return to New York on April twentieth. Do you think you can handle it?" she snapped.

John, not wanting to show he was terrified of changes, replied, "Yeah, why not?"

They packed, boarded, and settled in for a relaxing cruise. A problem arose five days after they had sailed from New York when they arrived in Cartagena, Colombia. John was taking keen notice of the street whores, pimps, and scum that inhabit the crevices of any city. As a former New York City cop he was able to pick out these lowlifes while they went unnoticed by everyone else. He was surprised to discover that the reminder of the power he had once wielded had sexually aroused him.

John Ryan realized that he missed the job. That night he confronted Mary and insisted that she accommodate him in fantasy sex play. Mary, who was having the best time of her life, relented. She was so happy to be sailing among the rich and famous, and she was being treated like a queen herself.

It wasn't so bad, Mary thought after her husband had blind-folded her, tied her to the bed in their cabin,and had proceeded to talk roughly to her. His sex performance had been satisfying, and he didn't appear to drink as much as he normally did the following day. He was actually courteous to the other couples seated at their tables in the luxury ship's Mauretania Restaurant.

After the first such encounter in their cabin Ryan continued with his sex routine every night for two weeks. He then slacked off to performing every other day, then to twice a week, and by the time they reached Hong Kong in March, he was down to a once-a-week ritual.

It was 1 April and the ship was sailing toward Walvis Bay, Nambia, on the west coast of Africa; John Ryan felt the surge of power well up inside him. He kneeled on the bed over the helpless female form. She was tied spread-eagle to the bed, and for his further stimulation John had wrapped her tightly in plastic wrap that he had gotten from his waiter. The tight, smooth softness of the clear wrapping around her body increased the sensation of power within him. The fogging on the inside of the airtight enclosure urged him to greater energies. The gag and blindfold around her face further increased the helplessness of his victim.

She rocked from side to side, moaned, and appeared to arch her body in violent bursts. John assumed her motion was pleasure. He kept her this way for more than an hour, and then he noticed her movement slowed. He was getting tired too, so he took a break and went to the bathroom, leaving her in the helpless position. He took his time, even deciding to shower, feeling comfort in the knowledge of the power he had over a female again.

When he emerged from the bathroom he noticed she wasn't moving. He shook her, unbound her motionless body, and unraveled the plastic wrap. He felt a sense of terror when he realized she was quite dead. With his cabin located on deck 5, far below the waterline, it would be too complicated to throw her overboard. He could never get her body out of the cabin without being seen; the cabin steward's office was right outside.

"Why am I so panicked?" he thought. This was an accident.

**22**

When Ryan realized it was not a crime, he decided he had nothing to worry about, so he called the medical facility.

The ship's doctor realized Ryan's embarrassment at having death occur to his wife of twenty-five years during sex-play. Although the poor woman looked much younger than her nervous husband did, he did his best to comfort this man. Dr. Michaels asked if his wife had a history of any medical or heart problems. Ryan indicated no, but reminded the doctor of the case of the gonorrhea he had passed on to her several years before.

"I told her I caught it from a toilet seat, and she was dumb enough to believe it," he explained to the confused doctor.

"What about your wife's family, was there any history of heart disease?" the doctor queried.

"What does my wife's family have to do with this?" Ryan asked the doctor.

"I am just concerned about whether there may be a genetic passage of a medical abnormality," the doctor replied. At this point the doctor realized the great embarrassment Mr. Ryan was suffering, so he told him he would continue the questioning after they had removed the body of his wife to the medical facility.

"Oh!" Ryan exclaimed with a slight smirk. "You think this is my wife?"

Puzzled, Dr. Michael placed his hand on top of his bald head and immediately acquired a blanched expression. "Then who is this poor woman?" asked the stunned ship's doctor.

"I don't remember her name, but she sits at our table in the Mauretania," replied a drunken John Ryan. "Do you think we could say she fell down the stairs so Mary doesn't find out?"

# The Weak Heart

Molly Steiner was blessed with a remarkable body. She didn't realize it until her sophomore year at Midwood High School in the Flatbush area of Brooklyn.

She would soon learn from her gymnastics coach to make the most of that perfect body. The high school, located on Avenue H across the street from Brooklyn College, was known for its well-mannered, mostly Jewish student population. Among its notable alumni were Woody Allen and Sy Syms.

Molly was also known for her remarkable feats of athletic prowess. She was a favorite of the physical education department and a natural at gymnastics. Her area of expertise was the balance beam. Her only previous training had been at ballet school when she was nine years old. Molly had hated ballet because all she had heard from the instructor was criticism. Since she had become a gymnast all she had heard from her coach was praise. The balance and grace Molly displayed on the beam was without parallel. In her junior year she won the New York City PSAL individual championship on the beam.

Molly was always in the physical education office when not in class. Patty Sammartino, her gymnastics coach, a muscular physical education teacher who walked with a mannish sway, was her mentor in all things. Sammy, as Ms. Sammartino was affectionately called, had been suspended from school once for punching a male student out cold. The superintendent did not accept her defense that the student, a black member of the football team from Bedford Stuyvesant, had fondled her ample breasts while she passed through the crowded hallway between classes. Molly thought she wanted to quit school when she heard what had happened to Sam. She missed her company and guidance terribly. She also missed Sam's continual compliments about her voluptuous body, ramrod straight skeletal structure, and smooth complexion. It was at this time that a close friendship formed between the student and coach. Molly frequently visited Sammy at her apartment on Stanton Street, located on the lower East Side of Manhattan. The basic tenet that Sammy lived by was, "All men suck." Molly, who respected Sam, made that her motto, too. Sammy's suspension lasted six weeks, and when she returned to school all males, students and teachers alike, gave her a wide berth when she passed in the halls. Nonetheless, she was given a hero's welcome. No one was happier to have her back than Molly.

Bernie Bunstein was in his last year as Midwood High School's language department chairman. He had given the Board of Education thirty-five years of his sweat and blood, and he looked forward to retirement. Bernie was not a popular educational leader. He walked with a stooped posture, and his slender face, preceded by a long, hooked nose garnished with protruding nostril hairs, earned him the nickname "Ratface." Howard Newman, the multitalented teacher from the physical education department, had once said, "Ratface has more hair growing out his nose and ears than he has on his head."

Ratface was continually snooping into the personal lives of his language teachers, whose teaching skills he always found lacking. He despised his female teachers most. He remembered years ago when, fearful for their jobs, they would not hesitate to answer his departmental personal questionnaire, but then, in the late seventies, a particularly articulate French teacher who was married to a recently elected member of the New York State Assembly refused to answer the question regarding her menstrual cycle. She indicated that it was private information which she would rather not disclose. Mr. Bunstein said he needed to know so that his female teachers would not take days off related to their periods.

"Can't you understand, its for the good of the department," he snarled at her. The poised and confident professional held her ground. When Bernie told the principal he wanted to get rid of this teacher, Ratface was informed that she had a connection to a powerful rabbi at 110 Livingston Street, the headquarters of the New York City Board of education. With great disappointment he also found out that the principal did not approve of his questionnaire, and he was ordered to abolish the use of it. Bernie then seethed with hatred for yet another group; along with blacks, gays, lesbians, physical education teachers, goym, and Hasidim, Bernie Bunstein also hated democrats.

How the strange relationship between Bernie and Molly began is not well documented. Molly, some said, acquired Bernie as a massage client; others say she became his personal trainer after his second heart attack. All that is known to be factual is that there was a marriage between the cranky, foul-smelling, sixty-five-year-old retired educator, Bernie Bunstein, and lithe, graceful, sweet, twenty-five-year-old Molly Steiner. The New York Times society page carried the story, which was notable because of Bunstein. The column in the Times was not printed because of Bernie's educational successes, which were nil, but because of his grandfather who had invented the Bunsen burner, used in so many laboratories, and the source of his great fortune.

The honeymoon was to be a round-the-world cruise on the QE 2. The luxury ship, the pride of the famed British Cunard Line, began its

Millennium World Cruise on 4 January 2000, and would return to New York on 20 April 2000.

Bernie Bunstein prided himself on his awareness of his environment. He was challenged beyond belief on the QE 2. He tried to memorize the lettered stairways and their destinations. He remembered that the stairways and elevators were lettered from A to H from forward to aft. The main stairways were A, E, and G. The main accommodation decks were numbered one to five. Odd-numbered rooms were on the starboard side, and even numbered rooms were on the port side. Since Ratface had never been on a ship before he had to learn that starboard was the right side and port was the left side. The confusion soon overwhelmed Bunstein and quickly added the Cunard Line to his hate list.

The stresses were quickly forgotten when he was in the company of his loyal, twenty-five-year-old, statuesque wife. She always encouraged him to try the new and varied foods that were on the menu. The accommodations that went with their three-hundred-thousand-dollar cabin allowed them to dine at the posh Queen's Grill. After dinner Molly would insist that he relax with a cigarette at the table, followed by a cigar and brandy in the Chart Room. Bernie had quit smoking years ago, but Molly said she wanted him to be happy and encouraged him to indulge in the obscene habit, as Sammy referred to it. Because of her stunning good looks Molly was often the center of male attention wherever they went. She would often reassure Bernie that she would always be loyal to him and that no other man would ever have her. She told him he should feel flattered he had such an attractive wife, reminding him of the usual dessert that was in store for him when they retired to their luxurious cabin.

At this point Molly would order him another drink and insist that he finish it. She knew the excess of smoking and drink would be disturbing to Bernie's doctor after his two heart attacks, but the putz doctor was not in line to inherit the double-digit millions when Bernie died.

Molly knew that the combination of Viagra, methamphetamine, blood pressure medication, and single malt scotch would have the desired results. Sammy had told her so. She increased the dosage of each night after night, but to her dismay his bedtime activity always seemed to increase. She would fall asleep before he did, and sometimes Ratface would get dressed and return to the Chart Room and sing the praises, to any bar patron who would listen, of the Viagra cocktail his young wife would mix for him every night. "Aren't you afraid she will kill you, Bernie?" a heavy drinker once asked him. "She is worth it," he replied with a sly smirk. "What a way to go!"

It happened while crossing the date line as the ship was approaching Lautoka, Fiji. The call from the frantic-sounding companion to the medical facility indicated a serious health emergency. A competent medical team was quickly dispatched to the posh suite on the boat deck. After a thorough examination, it was determined that there was no pulse and no breathing. Cardiopulmonary resuscitation was administered. After twenty minutes Dr. Granger announced to the sad and nervous-looking spouse that it must have been an aneurysm because death had been instantaneous and nothing could have been done. The doctor was quite mournful, as was the entire medical team. It was well known that this was a honeymoon cruise and the couple had been married for only a month. "It was so tragic," they all agreed.

The next night the conversation at the bar in the Chart Room, the favorite hangout of Bernie Ratface Bunstein, was about the effects of the Viagra cocktail.

"It's such a loss, because now no one will ever know what she put into it," Ratface moaned to his audience of somber fellow drunks.

# THE SECRET OF KUROMBO GAMA

The QE 2 was sailing westward toward Auckland, New Zealand, the weather was balmy and the sea was calm. Eighty-five-year-old retired school principal Kenji Ohara was seated in a comfortable deck chair at his favorite location, on the starboard side, forward on the sun deck. As the ship headed west toward the setting sun he pondered the dark secret that had festered within him for the last fifty-five years.

As an officer of the Japanese Imperial Navy during the war he had taught navigation to fledgling naval officers. He was proud of the glorious duty he had performed in the service of the Emperor. Kenji reflected upon his successful career and his abundant family. He had been a great-grandfather for the last ten years. All of his descendants were healthy, his sons were successful businessmen, and all had traditional wives. Aware of his fortunate and fruitful life, he tried to shake the recent discomfiting thoughts from his mind.

Arnold Riddick, the handsome, retired New York City high school principal seated at Kenji's table was the age of his oldest son, Shinsea. He had white hair both at his temples and speckled throughout his neatly trimmed beard, and his erect posture showed evidence of a trim, athletic lifestyle. This black American was a reminder of the vile event that had occurred during the unpleasant days of the occupation of his homeland at the war's end. The face and body posture of Principal Riddick were familiar to Kenji. He had seen them before in the village of Katsuyama on a night in 1945. It was an occasion he wanted to forget.

Each night since they had left New York Harbor on 4 January 2000, Kenji had been disturbed by memories of the past. The horrible recollections of that time so long ago had begun at the beginning of this Millennium World Cruise. Since they had first been seated for dinner in the Mauretania Restaurant located on the upper deck, upon meeting this American, he could not get the secret of Kurombo Gama from his mind.

It was not as though this gentlemanly, retired principal and his lovely wife fit into the evil memories of half a century ago. It was the familiarity of this black American's appearance that shook Kenji. He was haunted by the memories of the horrors of the war's end. Kenji remembered the brutality of the occupying black marines.

The all-black Thirty-seventh Marine Depot Unit had been trained at Monford Point, North Carolina, apart from the regular marines. The Marine Corps was racially segregated until 1948, and the marines stationed near Katsuyama as part of the occupying military force were not gentle with the Okinawan populous. The women were often raped. On a typical weekend several armed marines would come by jeep to the outlying village and demand women for their sexual pleasure. Typically a screaming woman would be carried off into the fields to be raped repeatedly. The marines from the Thirty-seventh Depot Unit would bring food and beer and remain for many hours and sometimes for the entire weekend. An Okinawan woman who did not cooperate would be beaten. This practice was so widespread that many pregnancies had to be terminated from these horrible encounters. On some occasions the pregnancies would be allowed to go full term in the hope that the baby would prove to be descended from the Okinawan husband. Great anxiety would occur until the newborn baby could be viewed. If the baby was unmistakably multiracial, he or she would be killed.

As Okinawans they were told to act in a manner befitting a conquered nation. The Emperor and his government were allowed by General Douglas MacArthur to continue to rule so long as the Japanese people acted with honor, and maintained the status of a conquered people. It was said that MacArthur was a fair man and had the good of the Japanese economy at heart. He was enacting reforms to abolish the Japanese feudal and military system and promised future greatness for Japan. There was no reason to distrust the American general, for he was known to be a man of honor.

Marine Privates Floyd Jones from Columbus, Ohio, Reggie Jefferson from Gary, Indiana, and Bobby Gordon from Augusta, Georgia, all pulled guard duty on that weekend in July 1945. By trading cigarettes and a bottle of gin, the three buddies were able to get their weekend liberty. They knew where they wanted to go; they had been there before. The village of Katsuyama just past Nago was their target. The women were compliant, and the men were suckers. They had enjoyed themselves there on previous occasions, and the three marine privates were anticipating another weekend of excitement.

The privates would not be able to bring their weapons, because they were supposed to be on guard duty. First Sergeant Russell Edmunds did not know other marines were covering their assignments. Had he known of these plans he would have thrown the three in the brig, for he was known for his intolerance of any behavior that would bring shame upon the United States Marine Corps. Had the weapons been missing from their racks, First Sergeant Edmunds would surely have noticed for he always counted them. They didn't need weapons anyway; the three of them outweighed the entire male population of the village. Private Floyd Jones, their leader, had it all planned well. It would be a weekend to remember.

They were right. The weekend would be well remembered, but not for the brutal sex party they had planned. It would not be remembered for the beating of the unwilling girls, for tying them up to trees to secure them and for awakening them to fulfill the continual sexual demands made upon them. This occasion would be indelibly imprinted in many memories for other reasons for more than half a century. The horrible memories would continue to replay for fifty-five years, and would stretch to the sun deck of the QE 2 on the Millennium World Cruise, even to 5 February in the year 2000.

That night at dinner Kenji Ohara knew he must question Mr. Riddick about his past. "Have you ever researched your genealogy, sir?" asked the Japanese educator.

"Not really," replied the New York educator.

"You obviously have African ancestry," Ohara pried.

With a chuckle Riddick said, "That's for sure."

"What about your beginnings in the United States. Were your ancestors slaves?"

"I am from a long line of cotton pickers," was the reply, with another chuckle.

"How long has your family been in New York?"

"Since the 1940s. Why do you ask?" Riddick was curious.

"Because, Mr. Riddick, I knew a marine in Okinawa fifty-five years ago who looked exactly like you. Did your father serve in the armed forces in World War II?"

"No, not my father. He was blinded in one eye as a child. He was four-F."

"Four-F?"

"Yes, the draft board would not accept men who were classified physically incapable for combat," said Riddick, who was wondering why this Japanese man was so inquisitive.

"There was an American marine who was part of the occupation forces that often came to our village who looked exactly like you," Ohara explained.

"Well, I took a racial sensitivity course in college a few years ago, and we learned there that people who are not familiar with other races often remember only distinctive differences of that unfamiliar race. Skin color, body posture and shape, and facial configurations all appear to be similar to a foreign culture. You probably saw the first Negroes of your life. Dey say we alls look alike," Riddick joked.

Ohara did not laugh. He replied with a bow of his head, "I apologize if I have offended you."

After dinner, Kenji and Oshi walked on the boat deck amid the eerie blue-white glare from the stars of the southern hemisphere. He said to her, "I am familiar with many races. I know the subtle differences in their characteristics. I am convinced he is related to that marauder."

"Does that place him at fault if he is?" Kenji's wife Oshi asked.

"Of course not, but if he is I must tell him of the secret of Kurombo Gama. It is tearing away my insides," responded an anguished Kenji.

"Then you must talk to him."

The next night in the Mauretania Restaurant Kenji steered the conversation toward his homeland. This was easy to do because the other women at the table always had questions regarding Oshi's traditional attire. Kenji explained that their homeland of Okinawa was the main island in the Ryukyu Island chain, which is scattered in a southwesterly direction from the southernmost Japanese island of Kyushu. The Ryukyu chain extends to Taiwan in the East China Sea. He went on to explain that his homeland enjoyed the best and worst of both Chinese and Japanese culture. Around 1600, China replaced its civil envoys with military men. Around 1500, King Hashi of the Okinawan Sho dynasty united the Ryuku Islands into one kingdom. To ensure rule by law and to discourage political rivals, he seized all weapons in the kingdom and made possession of a weapon a crime against the state. Punishment for ownership of any weapon was death. About two hundred years later, Okinawa became part of the domain of the Satsuma clan of Kyushu, and again a weapons ban was stressed. As a direct result of these successive bans, it is said the art of empty-handed self-defense called Okinawa-te was developed.

"Do you mean karate?" asked a diner, held in fascination at this story.

"Exactly," replied Kenji. He continued explaining that Funakoshi Gichin, born in 1869 in Shuri, Okinawa, systematized this form of empty-hand combat into the modern-day karate. In July 1945, a month before the atom bombs were dropped on Hiroshima and Nagasaki, his homeland was occupied by a Negro marine detachment. Kenji went on to explain, without much detail, the horrors his family and neighbors suffered.

Kenji then explained the secret of Kurombo Gama. As the village became desperate about the systematic raping of their wives, mothers, and daughters by a handful of the same black marines, they sent for Saburo Tanamachi, a fisherman with only one eye. "Very much like your father, Mr. Riddick," Kenji said, holding the attention of everyone at the table. Saburo was a master karate sensi, a disciple of

Funakoshi Gichin. Some of the men of the village had decided to end the terror they had been suffering.

The incident occurred on the weekend when the cocky marines had come to the village unarmed. When they arrived they made their usual demands. This time a one-eyed fisherman politely asked them to leave. The three marines were far bigger than the slight, humble Saburo. One of the privates was the size of a sumo wrestler. It was this huge, towering barbarian who first approached Saburo. Private Jefferson attempted to grab Saburo around his neck. The fisherman's movement was so fast that the other marines could not understand what had caused Reggie to wind up face-down on the ground.

"What da fuck you do?" Private Gordon shouted to Saburo, who understood no English. The speed of Saburo's deadly choku-zuki strike left the two marines dumbfounded. The frightened villagers who witnessed the strike to the solar plexus of Private Jefferson, Thirty-seventh Marine Depot Unit, United States Marine Corps, were also not sure what they witnessed.

As Gordon approached Saburo there was another lighting strike. This time it was a shuto-uchi to the side of the neck of the hapless marine, who immediately joined his comrade in convulsing on the ground with his face in the red Okinawan mud. Private Jones foolishly thought the slightly-built man had gotten in a lucky punch which he had not seen and he charged straight toward the one-eyed man. Jones never reached his target; he thought he saw the man turn sideways, raising his knee. He never saw or felt the yoko-geri-keage as the side of the fisherman's foot struck his throat.

Upon seeing their hero, Saburo Tanamuchi, render the three bullies helpless, the villagers ran to the three bodies on the ground and quickly set about beating them to death. Their efforts were wasted on Jefferson, for he was already dead.

A donkey cart appeared and the bodies were loaded on board. The trip to the cave, which became known as Kurombo Gama, took nearly an hour. "Kurombo Gama means, "The Cave of the Negroes,'"

Kenji explained. The bodies were dropped into the depths of the grotto, and their remains were left there.

The diners at table 28 in the Mauretania Restaurant were astonished. Soft-spoken Irma Riddick broke the silence. "Those must have been terrible times."

"Indeed they were, and you see, they still are," Kenji replied. "My wife Oshi here suffers from ovarian cancer. She does not expect to see the end of this cruise. We believe her illness was brought on by an infection she received when she was raped as a young teen."

# THE DAME

Carol Cortland was ninety-eight years old but felt as if she were only twenty-eight. Referring to her age, she told her fellow passengers on the Queen Elizabeth 2 Millennium World Cruise 2000, "It is only a number." This was her eighth consecutive world cruise and she knew the ship better than most staff members did. She traveled with her entourage, which included Fifi, her Pekinese, who had to remain in the ship's comfortable kennel, and Wilma Thomas, her nurse and best friend. Dame Carol Cortland felt fortunate to have her closest living friends with her on this cruise. Enrico Cuchiara, her competent chauffeur, had remained home to administer her three-hundred-acre estate in Herfordshire and to care for her twin Rolls Royces. She possessed the secure feeling of having a home to which she could return. Dame Carol was a content woman.

Carol, which is what she insisted upon being called by her servants, had enjoyed a successful career as a writer of children's books. It was said she was the most successful children's writer ever, and her career had lasted nearly sixty years. Her heroines were always wide-eyed, idealistic, and filled with a drive to right the societal wrongs that she so aptly depicted in writing about the world through a child's eyes. Her heroes, and there always was one to admire, were handsome, charming, well mannered, and had the admirable physical characteristics and mannerisms of her father.

By the time she was nineteen, she had turned down three marriage proposals from members of English gentry. After the success of her first novel in 1925, she lived on the left bank of Paris with successful New York playwright Eva K. Flint, who was basking in the glow of her recent hits, Subway Express and Under Glass. They lived together in a cold-water flat well beneath their means, smoked pot, drank wine, hung out in the cafes frequented by aspiring artists and writers, and had a great time. They allowed as yet unknown notables such as Bennett Cerf, F. Scott Fitzgerald, and Noel Coward to flop in their pad when these artists didn't have the financial means to sustain themselves.

She married Douglas Farnsworth Lancaster, a prosperous Welshman, who became known for his archeological pursuits throughout the world. They had three children—two daughters and a son—none of whom did a thing to support themselves, ever. Dame Cortland's children were lazy, spoiled, and selfish. She was much happier in the company of her lapdog and her servants whom she continued to outlive. She never saw much of her husband, who was often somewhere on the globe where there was a historical dig in progress, one which he generally would be financing. When Douglas died in 1961, Carol said, "This will create a cavity in my life about the size of the one in my tooth," referring to how little she had seen him.

Dame Carol gave huge sums of money to her favorite charities, the first of which was the Antivivisection League of Great Britain, popular in the 1920s. This was replaced by the animal rights organization People for the Ethical Treatment of Animals, currently favored by French actress Brigitte Bardot as well as many other artists of the stage and screen.

Dame Carol knew her selfish children had been waiting for her to die for nearly half a century. Their desire for the estate to fall into their hands was quite transparent. Each of the indolent offspring had retained barristers to contest her will. They each felt that they deserved a greater share than either of their siblings.

Wilma Thomas had been with Dame Carol for twenty-two years, and had catered to the desires and needs of her mistress with great pleasure. Wilma, fifty-six years old and a native of Jamaica, was widowed at the age of thirty. She had come to England seeking employment as a domestic servant. Her formal displays of respect and affection had earned her high praises. Dame Carol had heard about her and had offered a lucrative contract. Wilma had explained that she had never finished high school, so Dame Carol, who had an eye for character, had offered to send her to school. Wilma, with her cafe au lait complexion, tall slim figure, and warm winning smile, had gladly accepted. Both women could not have been happier with the long-lasting arrangement.

Despite Wilma's dark past in Jamaica, where she had received a suspended sentence for the killing of her abusive husband, Dame Carol had been happy to take a chance with her. She had hoped that Wilma's background would even be an advantage. The source of many female domestic servants' problems were the men in their lives; Dame Carol correctly presumed that Wilma would not have any such emotional involvements. The fact that Wilma had cut her husband's throat while he was in a drunken sleep hours after he had beaten her did not shake Dame Carol's confidence in her.

Dame Carol couldn't be happier with Wilma. Wilma's days off were mostly spent on the estate, playing with and caring for the dogs, cats, and horses. She and Dame Carol had slept together every night Carol's husband had been away, which had been often, and Wilma had never asked for or demanded anything from that relationship. When they made love Dame Carol often thought of her carefree youth in Paris so many years ago.

It was April, nearly midnight, and Wilma Thomas was sitting in the Yacht Club aboard the QE 2 approaching Lisbon. The Yacht Club was a comfortable disco lounge located on the upper deck astern. Wilma was listening to the sounds of Opus playing hits from the '60s and '70s. The quartet was also from Jamaica, and the thoughts of her earlier life there made her shudder. Wilma realized how much she would miss Dame Carol.

Earlier that day, news of Dame Carol's passing had reached the ears of her greedy children. They each in turn had notified their attorneys to begin proceedings to settle the estate. Two yachts, a twin-engine Piper aircraft, and a Ferrari, had already been ordered by the Dame's presumptuous offspring. Each one was determined to garner a larger share of the estate than the other two. Each one was convinced he or she deserved more. All three were due for a rude shock.

As Wilma sat enjoying the soft rock sounds of Opus, she pondered the massive coup that had been engineered by Dame Carol. In the ship's Safe Deposit Centre located on deck 2, stairway G, the Dame's will waited. Much to the surprise of her three offspring, the will turned the entire estate grounds over to the RSPB, the Royal Society for the Protection of Birds. It stipulated that Enrico should be given one Rolls Royce and his present quarters over the garage. The will also stipulated that Dame Carol's best friend and lover, Wilma should remain on as administrator of the estate and be given the other Rolls Royce and the sum of one million pounds. The RSPB, with Bill Oddie, prominent British TV personality, named as administrator, would receive the remainder of Dame Carol's securities, valued at about twelve million pounds. Furthermore, the RSPB would be charged with planting the three hundred or so acres with vegetation that would both conform best to the natural environment and also afford the birds a continuing resource of food and shelter.

Wilma eyed the enigmatic, tuxedo-clad man whose chest was adorned with a dozen or so military medals. His shaved head accentuated his dark goatee. The fact that he was sitting alone aroused an interest in Wilma she had thought was forever gone. He did not seem to notice Wilma's approach. The sensual swaying hips of Betty Jones, Opus' lovely lead singer, captivated him as she moved with the rhythm of her music.

Wilma went over to the mysterious stranger and asked him to dance. With a broad smile he gladly accepted.

# Plain Jane

Her fatigue was underscored by the lack of arm motion when she walked. She had short, helmet-shaped, straight gray hair as did many of the mental patients of the 1940s. Dark, satchel-like bags were prominent under sad gray eyes that never seemed to look at anyone. Her sagging shoulders accentuated her slim frame. Jane Bland was sixty-two years old, but could have passed for a sad seventy-two. She always wore calf-length, shapeless dresses with little color that hung on her frail frame like clothes on a hanger. The most noticeable element of her sartorial nonsplender was her footwear. She wore white Adidas Supernova running shoes. Jane wore those shoes everywhere; she even wore them with her pale blue gown to the captain's reception. If someone had asked her why she always wore running shoes she would have told them about the torsion bar in the midsole that gave her protection from the pain of her annoying heel spur. No one ever asked, though. The devastating characteristic of Jane's semblance was that it seemed that she just didn't care. She didn't care about life, her family, or this boring QE 2 world cruise her worried daughters had arranged for her.

The passengers on the QE 2 could not help but notice the wispy, bored-looking woman who never smiled. Jane was often seen at afternoon tea in the Queen's Grill, amidships on the quarterdeck, at four o'clock. She would sit alone, listening to the music of the talented harpist Maria Banks. If a curious passenger spoke to her to she always responded politely with one-word answers. Jane made it clear that she didn't want to be included in conversation.

She was also seen walking on the boat deck in the early

morning. Jane would walk outdoors for an hour every morning, in all kinds of weather. She would then have a buffet breakfast in the Lido after finding an empty table where she could sit alone. Jane enjoyed the sunrise more than anything, because it gave her hope for a better day. Unfortunately, it never seemed to come.

Seth Bland was all that Jane had ever cared about, ever since they had met, which was after the game against Texas A & M. Back then, Jane was a senior cheerleader at the University of Texas known for her gymnastic abilities, and Seth was freshman quarterback whose emerging talents promised a pro career. Seth played in the last quarter that day because of an injury to starter Jim Kelly. Seth's ninety-nine-yard touchdown pass to Tim Evans set a team record and gave them a win. The rivalry against the "Aggies" was a bitter one, and Seth was the hero. He went on to a pro career, playing for the Oakland Raiders, married Jane, had two daughters, and enjoyed the good life that came with being a sports hero. If he had stayed healthy his career would have gone on for many years.

Seth did not stay healthy; he went bad in a big way. Although his physical machine stayed intact, his character fell apart. Some said it was gambling that destroyed him. Others said it was drugs. With self-destructive habits like those, his career was destined to fail. He owed the Las Vegas bookies big bucks, and they were quite pleased with their windfall. Seth hesitated when they wanted him to shave points because he thought he could raise money a better way. He was wrong.

Seth made a copy of the Raiders playbook and attempted to sell it to J. D. Roberts, the New Orleans Saints' coach. A playbook has the closely guarded secrets of a team's offensive and defensive plays, and is highly valued in the world of football. Roberts reported the offer to the NFL security office.

The league notified FBI agents, who arranged to be present at the predawn meeting in a New Orleans parking lot where the exchange was to take place. Seth was charged with wire fraud and interstate transportation of stolen property. Seth, having finished his promising career, was also finished with his life as a family man. While he was in the grasp of alcohol and drugs, Jane divorced him.

It was at this point in her life that Jane ceased being the graceful, pert college coed whose identity never left her. She entered into a depressed state, clinging to the hope of returning to her previous life with Seth. Jane lived for the rare visits Seth had with his daughters. When she got to see him, she always hoped that he had changed, and when she realized he was still strung out on drugs, her heart would sink a bit lower than its previous level.

Jane's daughters insisted she go on the Millennium World Cruise 2000 which left New York Harbor on 4 January 2000 and was scheduled to return on 20 April. They thought it would raise their mother's sagging spirits.

Unknown to Jane while seated at her table for six in the Mauretania Restaurant was that she was often the object of conversation among her other five dining companions. Arnold Fayne and Joel Gorsky, both in their early forties, had been living together for ten years. Because of the men's unusually good looks, single women often stopped in midsentence when they passed. Arnold was six-feet-two with a body-builder's frame; his shining, wavy black hair was offset by distinguished white temples. Joel was of equal height, but his frame contrasted with Arnold's in that he had the appearance of a balding marathon runner. He was, in fact, emaciated.

Jane's first effort at conversation was prompted by her curiosity about the numerous pills Joel took with his dinner. Convinced that these

51

two stunningly good-looking men were health enthusiasts, Jane asked, "What kind of vitamins are you taking?"

Out of earshot of the other diners, Joel answered, "This is medication. You see, Arnold and I are HIV positive."

Jane was immediately sorry she had asked and she attempted to apologize, but she was interrupted by Joel, who intimated that Arnold might have a normal life span but that his own level of health was beyond hope. Sadly, this was to be Joel's last cruise.

Jane was stunned, and it showed. Her plain, normally unchanging facial expression finally softened. She felt the tender emotions of caring and compassion. Jane felt as though a magician had snapped his fingers and said, "Wake up!" She wanted to hug them both. A stranger confiding to her a secret such as this had struck her with the impact of a lightning bolt. She felt alive again; her motherly instincts instantly permeated every cell in her body. All the love she had previously felt for her husband, who had needed her so much but had rebuffed her loving warmth, was now redirected.

The next morning, Jane visited the QE 2 health spa located on deck 7, stairway C, and was redirected to deck 1, stairway G, to the beauty salon when she realized that she was in the wrong place. She was in luck. She was able to get an immediate appointment. She had her hair styled and restored to its original chestnut brown. Jane also had a manicure and a Rene Guinot and Elemis facial. The makeover converted a once-devastated woman burdened by an unpleasant twist of fate to a phoenix reborn to youth.

The sea was rough after leaving Lisbon as the ship entered the Sea of Biscay off the coast of Spain. The diners at Jane's table in the Mauretania Restaurant that night thought their three missing companions were bothered by the weather and had chosen to skip dinner. They were wrong. The three were six decks below, in the ship's well equipped hospital. Joel was lying with tubes entering and emerging from various parts of his body. Jane held one hand as Arnold held the other.

Joel's last feelings were of happiness. With a smile he looked first at Arnold, his companion of so many wonderful years, and then at Jane. Joel felt responsible for the revival of an emotionally blank person who had now returned to her present state of happiness. His illness was the catalyst that had caused her metamorphosis. Confiding his personal burden to her had allowed Jane to feel needed again. Joel took his last gasp with a smile on his face.

Jane felt she now had a son. Arnold, a successful interior designer, postponed his flight home to LaJolla, California. He was going to spend a few days with Jane in Morristown, New Jersey, and help her to redesign her Victorian home.

Jane liked the feeling of being a surrogate mother. She was a new person.

Her daughters were ecstatic about their mother's transformation and would also be pleased that their instincts had been correct when they had sent Jane on the QE 2. It seemed Mother came home with more than a tan from the Millennium World Cruise.

# BODY AND SOUL

Jacques Baran was "launched,"—his word for born—on 1 November 1925. As a child he realized that he was not like other children, who were weaker and dumber than he. As a young man he represented France in the 1948 Olympics and won a bronze medal in track and field, at which time he was six-foot-one and a lean, muscular one hundred and seventy pounds. He had is name legally changed to FH 2025, for Future Human 2025, the number being one hundred years from that of his birth. He planned on living for a full century.

FH believed that with present medical advancements in the areas of transplants and artificial body parts, humans would soon be able to live at least one hundred years. In the event medical science should fail him, he had contracted with an organization in Scottsdale, Arizona, so that his body would be frozen at the time of death and placed in liquid nitrogen in a thermos tank at the Alcor Life Extension Foundation. It would take the greater part of his life's savings to achieve this end. Monsieur 2025's remaining assets would be left to his loving companion Rose. His expectation was that he would be restored when the medical technology to cure his fatal ailment became available. Realizing that no frozen mammal had ever been successfully thawed, he was nevertheless optimistic.

FH 2025 felt that future humans would be made up of mostly artificial body parts and would be able to engage in time travel. He was quite disappointed that he had missed his chance when the California cult successfully left earth with the Haley Bopp comet. FH knew they had achieved the ability to transport their souls through space. He anxiously awaited their return, because it would absolve him from the scorn he continually received for voicing his beliefs.

FH felt the concept of death was obsolete. He was also a believer in eugenics, and so thought that only the mentally worthy would have access to this life-prolonging technology. FH felt he belonged among the worthy.

FH 2025 had written several books explaining his theories and also taught at New York University, where he had many followers. He indicated his nationality as "citizen of the world" and believed that there should not be any political boundaries between countries. Although he had learned to speak English, French, Hebrew, and Farsi, he believed there should be a universal language. Mr. 2025 also believed strongly in one-world government.

Mr. 2025 was seventy-five years old when the QE 2 sailed out of New York Harbor on its Millennium World Cruise, and he felt in perfect health. When he boarded the ship he took no chances; he visited the captain to remind him that he must be immediately frozen in the event of his death. He was assured that his explicit directions would be followed.


Rose Anamamares was a few years younger than FH, her companion of thirty years. She did not look her age because she was the recipient of numerous surgeries to enhance her appearance. Rose checked into a clinic in North Carolina once a year for "upgrading." In the early 1970s she was at the cutting edge of breast augmentation. She had her boobs upgraded every time there was a new substance offered by medical science. Her face had been lifted so many times that she now had a permanent smile. This was broadened by the insertion of a facial underlayment. Placed beneath the surface of her face was a space-aged substance that formed an artificial chin, artificial cheeks and eyebrows, and an artificial nose. In addition, her lips received collagen injections six times a year, which gave them the appearance of the oversized wax lips children sometimes wear. Rose wore gluteal inserts to keep her buttocks as trim as a teenager's, and she had inserts to enhance her calves. Her midsection enjoyed the regular vacuuming of any and all adipose deposited there by nature. Her navel had been newly sculpted and she had been the recipient of a gynecological tightening.

These procedures were sometimes very painful, and occasionally Rose had to return for adjustments. In 1975 her breast implants became calloused and as hard as one's elbow; her nipples were so prominent that she was often asked if she was cold. On another occasion a cheek implant slid from its proper location and her face seemed to display symptoms of Bell's palsy. Rose didn't care that her friends and family knew she was mostly artificial; she lived for the "to-die-for" stares she received whenever she entered a new social environment.

For that reason, Rose loved cruises. Rose's presence always attracted attention on the ship. She had the appearance of a walking mannequin. Her platinum hair, Lord and Taylor wardrobe, and her body, laden with numerous pieces of jewelry, always raised the question of whether she was Mr. 2025's wife or daughter. Rose really loved cruises.

Rose had met FH when he was teaching at Long Island University in Brooklyn in the late 1960s. Rose was a waitress across the street at Junior's Restaurant. Jacques, along with his freaky beliefs, was a professor of quantum physics. She was attracted to his firm, quite weird beliefs. It was his offer to pay for augmentation surgery on her shamefully sagging breasts that had won her heart over. After the initial success with her breasts he offered to pay for a face-lift, and by then she was hooked.

The success of Rose's body realignment prompted FH to follow her into the world of plastic and silicone. They always seemed to be smiling when they were together. When Gary Macatangay, their Filipino cabin boy, entered their cabin early one morning without waking them, he noticed that they even slept with smiles on their faces.

FH 2025 died while in the QE 2 health and fitness spa. He was enjoying a therapeutic pool filled with seawater and heated to a perfect one hundred and three degrees with six high-pressure jet massage stations. FH was at Station One where the forceful water rises, swirling under the body with Niagara-like force. The sense of relaxation was overpowering as he lay flat on the wire holding-platform.

Rose was notified of a problem at 11:45AM just as her Legendary Trivia class was ending. She was asked to come to the purser's office. It was there that she learned that FH had passed away while undergoing hydrotherapy and had been found with a smile on his face. "He appeared to be quite happy, madam," Captain Wright told her.

"Well, what do we do now?" Rose asked.

Captain Wright explained that Mr. 2025 had requested that his remains to be frozen within fifteen minutes of his death.

"So can't we do that?" Rose inquired.

The captain went on to explain that Mr. FH had been in the hot water therapy pool for over an hour before he was discovered, because the smile on his face had indicated to the attendant that he had just been enjoying his bath. It was only when another guest asked FH to move to a different station that the situation had come to anyone's attention. When FH didn't move, a German passenger had become enraged and had formally reported the hogging of Station One. "You see, the German struck him out of frustration as Mr. 2025 seemed to ignore him and continued smiling. It was then that we realized Mr. 2025 was dead," the captain concluded.

Bridey O' Toole from the purser's office commented quietly to a coworker, "It seems so strange that a grieving widow would continue to smile like that."

"So," the captain asked, "what do we do with the body? It seems quick freezing is out."

"How much will it cost to fly him to Arizona in a frozen state?" asked Rose.

"Our next port is Durban. It would be in excess of a six-figured sum," the captain replied.

"Is there a less expensive way?" the Lord-and-Taylor bedecked woman meekly asked.

"Cremation would only cost several hundred dollars," the captain answered.

"He really wanted to be sent to that place in Arizona. I promised him," Rose murmured.

The Alcor Life Extension Foundation in Arizona soon received a UPS delivery with a letter explaining that the enclosed container held the ashes of FH 2025, a client of theirs. The letter asked whether he could be quick-frozen now. There was a paragraph about the QE 2, a hydrotherapy pool, Station One, and a German who mistook FH's smile. It made absolutely no sense to the overworked mail clerk, and he dropped the package into the trash bin.

# The Unsung Hero

Gerald Lipton was born in New York City on 1 October 1936. His parents had an apartment on Stanton Street located in the Jewish section on the lower East Side. His father, Harry, the son of Russian immigrants, was a cab driver. During World War II he had served aboard the HMS Seraph, the spy submarine that had been crucial during Operation Torch, the 1942 Allied landing in Algeria. In his early years, Gerry's father's nickname was "Bloody." Gerry didn't know why.

Gerald often told the story of his first recollection of his father's love for him. Harry had been home on a furlough and they were en route to the visit the Museum of Natural History. They were riding on a crowded subway car when seven-year-old Gerry stepped on a stranger's foot. The man backhanded young Gerry across the face. The slap was immediately followed by the sound of his father's fist, which instantly traveled to the man's jaw. There were two sounds from that day that remained forever imprinted in young Gerald's memory. The first sounded like a muffled firecracker. It came from the blow striking the bully's jaw and reverberated from deep inside his open mouth. The second sound, which appeared louder and more shocking to Gerald, was that of the man's head hitting the floor of the subway car. The dazed stranger lay there bleeding from the mouth, now missing his front teeth. Gerald and his father got off at the next station and resumed their journey by bus. While riding on the bus Harry told his son, "Gerry, when things in life get rough, you must learn not to panic." Gerry learned at an early age that different people have different ways of showing their love. He now knew why his father's nickname was Bloody.

Gerald remembered his father's love when the recon patrol of Hmung tribesmen he was leading was ambushed. There were twelve of them who had secretly landed in Laos to observe NVA activity in an area west of the Plain of Jars. Seven of his patrolmen were dead and the remainder were wounded. Gerry felt the AK-47 round enter his chest like a white-hot scalpel. As he lay there with his face resting in the grass he thought of his father's love and of that day on the subway. He felt the pressure of his blood building up in his lungs and he sensed he was about to die. He recalled his father telling him not to panic. The thoughts of home prompted him to rise from the damp earth and fire at the enemy. When he forced his body into a vertical position to fire his M-16 at the NVA, Gerry felt his lungs beginning to function properly again. He also felt renewed energy as his father's words repeated in his mind, "Don't panic, don't panic," and he moved from man to man, setting up a defensive perimeter. He gave encouragement to the men and directed their fire. Gerry's decisive action was later credited as being what had caused the NVA to withdraw. Had he laid there in the comfort of the cool, wet grass he would have drowned in his own blood, and surely they all would have perished.

Green Beret Lieutenant Gerald Lipton was told he could not be approved for the Medal of Honor, although his commander had attempted to nominate him. The reason was that had been were in a country where U.S. forces were not permitted to be. The regulations for this war, due to numerous convoluted political constraints, ruled out the Metal of Honor from being considered. Instead Lieutenant Lipton received his first of three Silver Stars and his first of four Purple Hearts. General Henry H. Shelton, the chairman of the Joint Chiefs of Staff, said of him in a White House ceremony, "He is an icon of what service in the armed forces is all about."

In 1966 Gerald was assigned to the Fifth Special Forces Group in Kontum Province, South Vietnam. This was a staging point for patrols into Laos and Cambodia seeking intelligence on North Vietnamese troop movements down the Ho Chi Minh Trail. Upon returning to the United States and his teaching job in Pershing Junior High School in Brooklyn, Gerry thought he could resume his career with the New York City Board of Education. He was happy to leave the madness of an undeclared war and the political deception it created and live a life of peace and normalcy. He would soon find out this was not to be.

In 1969 Gerald Lipton was transferred to a newly opening high school on suburban Staten Island. He was happy to get to the middle class area communities of Todt Hill and Castleton Corners. He also was glad to graduate to teaching a more sensible age group and to get away from the emotional instabilities of junior high school students. His license was for teaching Social Studies, but he didn't remain long in that position. Gerry possessed a unique personality that allowed him to calm even the most violent students and most unmanageable parents. Dr. Sam Altman selected him to be the number two administrator in the school with the title of Assistant Principal of Guidance, as part of what was later to become known as Pupil Personnel Services.

Gerald's talents did not go unnoticed in areas outside of his teaching profession. One of the teachers, Stanley Stempler, a member of the fledging Jewish Defense League, attempted to recruit his talented coworker. Gerry would have no part of it and rebuffed all advances to engage him. Gerald changed his mind when he met with the charismatic Rabbi Meyer Kouhani who introduced him to Israeli Captain Ari Levin. And so Gerald began his secret life as an undercover agent with the Mossad.

Luigi Ruggeri and his wife Aida were passengers berthed on the posh boat deck of the QE 2. When they boarded in New York on 5 January 2000, the husband and wife of fifty years looked at the three-hundred-thousand-dollar suite and wondered how they would manage for four months in such "close" quarters. Mr. Ruggeri had been a well known Swiss banker for half a century. His father-in-law, Arturo LeMole, founded the Istituto per la Industrale, a state holding company set up in the 1930s by the fascist Italian government to manage state properties. Mr. Ruggeri married the boss's daughter, and his international banking career was launched.

Luigi Ruggeri worked closely with the Fiat chairman Enrico Testa. In the 1980s Mr. Ruggeri helped the Testa family get rid of Libyan leader Colonel Mu'ammar al-Qaddafi as a shareholder in Fiat by buying back shares worth two-point-eight billion dollars. Mr. Ruggeri made the Testas even richer. Because of a complication in the financial arrangements, an international group of banks lost six hundred million dollars. This glitch did not affect Mr. Ruggeri's vast fortune, but he did lose power in the world of international banking.

Mr. Ruggeri thrived on power and worked to get it back. Iraqi leader Saddam Hussein needed a motivated international financial advisor, and Luigi Ruggeri was to be his man.

Well placed agents of the Mossad reported the imminent, unfriendly shift in international financial power. After much discussion among the operations section of the Israeli Intelligence Agency, a plan was formulated.

When Gerald Lipton received a visit at his winter home in Pembroke Pines, Florida, from General Ari Levin, he knew it was not a social call. He knew he would always say yes to being hired as a "consultant," whether by the U.S. Army or the Israeli intelligence branches. Since his retirements from the New York City Board of Education and the U.S. Army Reserve, Gerald had been saying "yes" about once a year.

Today was Gerry's day to run. He did six miles in forty-eight minutes. He alternated on workout days between running and body-building at the gym in his comfortable, gated community. Two nights a week he attended martial arts classes in nearby Hollywood. He was accomplished in most forms, his favorite being Kodokan Judo. Gerry was five-foot-ten and weighed one hundred and sixty pounds. He did five hundred sit-ups daily. He was in excellent physical condition.

While General Levin waited for Gerry's return from his run, he asked his lovely wife Joan if she would like an all-expense-paid, round-the-world cruise on the QE 2. These kinds of offers, Gerry knew, had entangling attachments, and they worried him. Joan, who was always supportive of him and accompanied him on all missions, insisted that they accept. He thought he was lucky to be placed undercover as a tourist and have his own wife travel with him. Most operations such as this utilized two agents. It seemed that Gerry was trusted enough to work alone.

The general explained that on one of the legs of the cruise, he didn't know which, a passenger might need special attention. Gerry was aware of the euphemisms used for assassination. Since he had done this work several times before, and since he loved excitement, he accepted. Joan, as on past assignments, would of course be told nothing of the mission. After all, she is a woman, Gerry thought. "The less women were told, the better.

Joan Babitsky Lipton, a retired school superintendent and a Rhodes Scholar recipient, was not known for any mental deficiencies. She knew of her husband's triple life as a successful educator and an intelligence agent for two countries, and she knew when to smile and gladly accept the offer of a trip on the QE 2.

The QE 2 Millennium World Cruise left New York Harbor on 6 January 2000 and sailed south to Miami. It then continued on to Cartagena, passed through the Panama Canal, sailed north, made two stops in Mexico and two stops in California, and then sailed westward to Hawaii. From there it sailed south for four days to Apia, Western Samoa. It crossed the international dateline on 1 February. Two more days of pleasant sailing brought the ship to Lautoka, Fiji. Then came New Zealand, where Gerry and Joan delighted at the Albatross that stayed with them for several days, reminding Joan of The Rime of the Ancient Mariner, which she had used in her English class at Pershing Junior High School in Brooklyn. Australia was followed with subsequent stops in Hong Kong, Bangkok, and Singapore. While in Hong Kong, Joan insisted that Gerry order a custom-made tuxedo with two waistcoats and accessories. As usual, when Joan insisted, Gerry was quick to comply.

At the next port, that of Colombo, Sri Lanka, Gerry received an email. He was asked by zedisded@aol.com to bring back some tea. It was at this moment that Gerry's vacation ended and his work began.

Gerry had had ten weeks to establish a rapport with Luigi Ruggeri. His task would have been made easier had the Mossad sprung for the more luxurious accommodations on the boat deck, but no, they had to scrimp according to their spartan budget. If it were such an important mission, you would think the Israelis would allot the funds, Gerry thought. General Levin explained that if certain negotiations were successful, Gerry would have no further function to perform other than enjoying a once-in-a-lifetime trip.

The accommodations Gerry and Joan had were located on deck 5, and Luigi Ruggeri's were on the boat deck, seven stories above him. What made matters more difficult was that they ate at different dining facilities, Joan and Gerry in the Mauretania Restaurant, and Ruggeri in the lavish Queen's Grill.

The dossier on Luigi Ruggeri that General Levin had brought to Florida indicated that Luigi, like Gerry, was addicted to exercise. A snap, thought Gerry. The health and fitness club, with its state-of-the-art Cybex weight machines, free weights, Stairmasters, treadmills, and Lifecycles, was always well utilized by the passengers. Gerry couldn't help but be amazed at the number of well informed people who exercised. In this situation he was sorry to see such a throng. He remembered the training he had received from the two intelligence services that demonstrated how people are usually oblivious to their surroundings. Gerry remembered to concentrate on the immediate task. He did.

Over the past ten weeks Gerry used his charm, intelligence, and personality to make an impression on Mr. Ruggeri. Gerry's physique, which showed the positive effects of proper diet, exercise, and living a happy life, gave the impression that he was a thirty-two-year-old athlete rather than a sixty-two-year-old retired educator. He moved with the grace of a cat. When Gerry gave advice in the gym, people listened.

Creatine monohydrate was the substance Gerry told Ruggeri was responsible for his excellent physical appearance. It really worked for building muscle tissue. Gerry gave some to Luigi who was soon hooked because the solution gave him the feeling of gaining strength. When the email message came in Colombo, Sri Lanka, all that had to be done was to supplement a normal packet of the Biochem Power Pump powder with time-release granules of concentrated epinephrine. The epinephrine had the effect of elevating the body's metabolic level. For a man's Luigi's age, the concentrated levels would be deadly.

Due to "political considerations," a euphemism which meant the decision was out of Gerry's hands and orders must be followed explicitly, the morning's email indicated that the "vitamins" had to be given that day. As Luigi expressed his satisfaction with the Power Pump powder containing creatine, Gerald realized this was the perfect time to give him the special packet. Gerry's heart almost fell into his jock when he realized he had picked up the wrong one. The packet in the pocket of his shorts was not the enhanced mixture containing the deadly dose of epinephrine. That packet had been left on the side of the bathroom sink.

Here was Luigi Ruggeri standing in front of him expecting to be given the packet that Gerry had promised him just a few minutes before. Ruggeri was in a hurry to leave. Gerry stalled by attempting to steer the conversation toward the next port's activities. Ruggeri wanted to leave, and Gerry could find no way to stall him any further without arousing suspicions. But the email indicated the dose must be given today. What was it his father had said eons ago about not panicking?

At that exact moment Joan arrived in a fashionable blue-and-white spandex aerobic suit, one Gerry had never seen before. In fact, Gerry had never seen Joan in this gym before. What was she doing here now he wondered? What timing!

Gerry thought desperately about how he might use this welcome diversion to delay Luigi. At that moment Joan asked, "Gerry, did you forget your vitamins this morning?" and she handed him the epinephrine-laced creatine packet.

"There it is," Gerry replied, with great relief. "I thought I had lost it."

As Mr. Ruggeri gratefully took the packet of vitamin powder, Gerry wondered about his wife. She always does turns up at the right time on these missions. Is it just luck, he thought.

Dr. Wright said that it had been a heart attack. Aida LeMole Ruggeri had always been against exercising and had told Luigi that he should rest in the morning instead of always going to those cardiovascular machines. "Figulo de putana," she murmured, "he never listened to me."

# SON OF SAM

Ronald Mazarolla was born on 10 October 1948. On Ronald's thirty-first birthday the first of the Son of Sam homicides occurred. During the summer of 1977, New York City was held in the grip of terror by a series of brutal murders. The New York Police Department was stymied and reached out to the public for information. Such was Ronald's character that three of his family members independently called the police department believing that Ronald was responsible.

As a child growing up, Ronald was, at best, a terrorist. His mother could not handle him except by bribing him. At the age of seven he had a charge account at the corner candy store so his insatiable demands could be met. If he did not get his way he would react with rage and violence. When he started kindergarten at St. Ephraim's Church he met with the immovable force of authority. Ronald learned at that early age that his power ended at the boundary of his immediate family. It was only his parents and his younger brother Vincent who could be bullied by him. The rest of the world must have known he was a fraud, as he could not manipulate them.

The one exception was sad Rosalie DiMarco. She was a neighbor who was learning disabled, and Ronald manipulated her into sexual activity when they were thirteen. A year later, in order to gain acceptance with the neighborhood boys, Ronald set up what amounted to a gang rape of sad Rosalie. When one of the boys told Father Trentino, the police became involved. Ronald's mother Jeannie blamed "that fat Rosalie retard," insisting that Ronald was innocent.

As Ronald grew older, his uncles, aunts, and cousins began to notice symptoms of dysfunctional behavior in the Mazarolla family. When his mother Jeannie called her brother John for help one day, the extent of the problem became evident. Her husband Sam could no longer put up with his son's behavior. His wife's lying overprotection of her dysfunctional son had forced Sam to move out. Apparently Jeannie was working two jobs to earn money to satisfy adolescent Ronald's demands for toys. It may have been an upgraded set of drums, a new target rifle, or a high-fidelity sound system. Uncle John drove to Brooklyn from Staten Island to assist his hysterical sister.

Sixteen-year-old Ronald had placed a noose around his neck, the other end of which was tied to a basement ceiling pipe, as he stood on a chair. He was threatening his mother with suicide if she didn't give him more money. He awaited Uncle John's arrival in the belief that he would write out a check as his mother had promised. Instead Ronald received his biggest disappointment since he had met his kindergarten teacher, Sister Mary Josepha. Uncle John, upon surveying the problem, attempted to kick the chair out from under the spoiled, manipulative Ronald. As he was falling Ronald quickly removed the noose from around his neck, revealing the nature of his bluff.

Jeannie continued to hide Ronald's transparent misdeeds. His younger brother Vincent, a shy, handsome, blue-eyed eleven-year-old, was very intelligent and received many awards for excellence in school. Ronald, who saw the birth of his younger brother as a threat to his controlling position in his family, was always plotting to discredit frightened Vincent. When Ronald gave his brother LSD to show Jeannie that Vincent was unworthy of her love, poor Vincent was hospitalized with hallucinations that reappeared throughout his life. Vincent was never the same after that episode. The already shy boy became withdrawn, quiet, and silent. He never smiled, nor did he ever initiate a conversation. He had become a broken child.

Ronald was proud of this deed, and Jeannie kept the incident from her family. When she told her estranged husband Sam of Ronald's acid caper, he returned to the Bensonhurst house on 74th and 10th Avenue and confronted his adolescent son. They were standing on the second floor landing outside the door to Ronald's bedroom when, with a great violent force, Ronald pushed his unsuspecting father down the flight of stairs. Sam's neck was broken. Due to Ronald's insistence, Jeannie didn't call the ambulance until all body functions ceased. The whole time poor Vincent sat quietly in his room with the door closed, staring at a balloon.

Ronald's first victim had been his father. Jeannie told the police she had been in a domestic dispute with her husband and that the fall was accidental. Ronald felt his talent at manipulation was natural, and he was proud of himself. Ronald had achieved sexual conquest, and now conquest over a person's life. He was sixteen and felt invincible.

Jeannie used the insurance money from Sam's death to send Ronald to the State University at Stoneybrook. When she read of a young girl's beaten body found in a wooded area on campus, she became worried about Ronald being at such a dangerous place. Jeannie was satisfied when she was able convince Ronnie to change colleges. He enrolled at the University of Florida in Gainesville.

When the news began carrying stories of decapitated victims found in Gainesville, Jeannie again worried that Ronnie was in a dangerous place. She wanted him to come home.

It took Ronald eight years to get a degree in engineering. By the time he graduated, his mother was in debt and there was a trail of bodies left in his wake. In 1975 he came home to live with his mother and his now heavily medicated brother. Ronnie never held a job for more than three months. He always felt the rejection of his coworkers. They couldn't stand to be around such arrogance. His supervisors saw through his feeble attempts to discredit his coworkers in order to advance his own cause. Ronald lacked all of the social skills necessary for normalcy.

In 1978 Ronald had to flee his Brooklyn home and become a fugitive. When he fired his .44 caliber revolver at his mother in an attempt to extract more money from her, the bullet passed through the wall of the house and embedded itself in the wall of a neighbor's house. The police were called and Jeannie denied everything. The neighbor showed the bullet to the police, and Ronald fled to California. He began collecting welfare and disability benefits based on phony symptoms he adopted that were identical to those of his poor hallucinating brother Vincent. The State of California was convinced and Ronald got an apartment in a welfare residency on Playa Del Sur facing the ocean in La Jolla.

In 1999 Jeannie died and her estate was settled. Ronald received forty-thousand dollars, his half of the estate. He was dissatisfied sharing with Vincent and wanted it all. His cousin, Angelo Mazarolla, executor of the estate and an attorney, explained it could not be done. Ronald said he was returning to New York to talk to his brother Vincent. Angelo told him, "Listen very carefully, Ronald. I remind you that we are descendants of Sicilians who have strict beliefs regarding family justice. There are two factions regarding you in this family. The liberals plan to kill you and make your body disappear. The older faction, namely your mother's brothers and sisters, plan to be harsher with you. When they finish with you they plan to dump your body in the tidal canals of Oakwood Beach so the crabs, rats, and eels will have a feast."

Ronald was dumbfounded. He knew his mother's family had identified him as a fraud since childhood. They had never believed his lies and false claims of greatness. He would have to rethink this inheritance.

Ronald read an article stating that cruise ships were filled with wealthy widows and divorcees. He decided he would use his powers of manipulation to achieve financial success on the high seas. He always knew he was destined for greatness, and now he would achieve that end. Ronald booked passage on the QE 2 Millennium World Cruise. He boarded on 19 January in Los Angeles.

Donna Vreeland was born in the upstate college town of New Paltz. Her father was a professor of economics. She grew up amid outdoor sports such as skiing, cycling, and mountain and rock climbing. In 1972, when she was a student at the university, she met and married Daniel Rosen. He was a serious fellow, tall, with curly blonde hair and a pear-shaped body. Everyone wondered how a man could have such narrow shoulders and such a wide ass. Donna graduated from nursing school and worked to support her husband Daniel who was a medical student. She was able to borrow money from a bank to secure his last two years' tuition. While he was a resident in a hospital in Phoenix, Daniel met a waitress and subsequently dumped Donna. He did not leave Donna empty-handed, though; she had the ten-year-old Volkswagen van under her name and his tuition loan which she would have to repay.

Donna was not a hateful person. She moved back to New York,

this time settling in Muncy Park on Long Island. As an operating room nurse at Manhasset Medical Center and with her reputation for no-nonsense competency, she was always in demand. Donna was always smiling. Her pleasant, dimpled face, which was mounted on a shapely five-foot-one-inch body, was framed with platinum hair. Her electric-blue eyes completed her angelic presentation. Donna never passed a homeless person in the street without asking if he or she needed anything, and always gave at least a dollar. She was never without friends and was always invited to parties and social gatherings.

At a barbecue at the home of a coworker from nearby Roslyn, Donna met Avi Galil. He was a computer technician from Israel desperately in search of an American wife. Donna, who was always willing to help a human in distress, married him and took out another loan to give Avi the money he needed to relocate in the United States. Donna's home in Old Westbury was ample enough for the two of them and was much more than Avi was used to having. They lived together for three years and Donna was quite happy until Avi told her about Remi, his other wife in Jerusalem.

That would not have been so bad, but Avi had two children, too. "Did you see her on those seven trips to Israel to visit your sick mother that I paid for?" she whined. The way Avi's eyes were constantly staring at his running shoes gave poor Donna another horrible thought. "You mean your mother isn't sick?" After more silent shoe study, she said, "You mean you have no mother?" Donna was devastated. As she became aware that she had been used as a doormat again, she began to cry.

Avi continued silently studying his shoes and then softly asked if he could have the house, saying Remi wanted to visit. Not believing what she was hearing, Donna looked up. "What?" she softly moaned.

"Maybe you could stay with a friend for a while. You see, Remi is a religious conservative and won't understand us being married. Please, just for a while," Avi begged.

Donna moved out the next day. She put her personal belongings in storage and moved to the town of Wingdale in Dutchess County. She immediately found employment at Harlem Valley Hospital.

After four years of watching the seasons change in the beautiful, semirural area of New York State located two hours north of the city, the smiling, dimpled, pleasant woman was again ready for another man. This time it was a wealthy retired physician whom she met at the fall semester gourmet cooking class at Dutchess Community College. Gilbert Marcus was the former head of New York City Hospitals. He had retired to his gentlemen's farm in Millbrook where he raised horses. He loved Donna's smile and aura of happiness, and they were married on the Fourth of July.

What could he take from me? she thought. He is so rich, and he can't steal anything from me, since I have nothing left.

In six months, poor Donna found out. Dr. Marcus was insecure about his younger, overly friendly, attractive wife. He insisted she tell him exactly where she was going every time she left the estate. One day he told her she could not leave the estate at all. She then realized that it was freedom that could still be taken from her.

Donna's first husband, Danny the Fanny, had taken her money. Her second, Avi the Israeli, had taken her house, and now she was a prisoner of Gil the pill. What is it about these circumcised husbands?" she thought. She vowed that from then on she would check for foreskins before she slept with a man.

On 6 January 2000 Donna Vreeland boarded the QE 2 at Pier 57 in New York Harbor. She looked forward to the fifteen weeks of luxury life aboard the Queen Elizabeth. She purchased the expensive package for three hundred thousand dollars, which gave her all of the available cruise comforts and residence on the boat deck. Unlike the lower cabins, from here she would have a view of the sea at all times.

It was 23 January, two days out of Honolulu on the Pacific Ocean, that she met the ruggedly handsome Ronald Mazarolla. He impressed her with all of his knowledge—of the sea, of wine, of dance steps, and actually, of any subject being discussed. She was amazed that he was always quite wrong. It didn't take long to realize that Ronald was really talking bullshit. She began to wonder if he had a foreskin.

When Ronald met Donna, he realized she was all he would ever want. Did she say she had received seventeen million dollars after the death of her husband, he greedily thought. Ronald knew he had made the right choice to invest his modest inheritance in this trip. He knew it would pay dividends. Donna was perfect for him. In a way he wished his mother were alive so he could flaunt his success at her.

Ronald began to plan about where they would live. Would they live in a coop on Central Park West in New York, or in a mansion over-looking the Narrows on Shore Road in Brooklyn? He then dreamed about the car he would get—either a Jaguar or a Ferrari. Why not both? he thought. The Jag would be silver and the Ferrari, red. Yes, life had just taken a turn for the better, Ronald mused.

Lying in Donna's bed located on the posh boat deck, with the moonlight reflecting on the blue Pacific through the porthole, Ronald began to discuss his plans with Donna. She must have been in agreement, he thought, because she said nothing. Ronald took her silence as acceptance. He told her how he was going to spend her money. He never suggested anything, he just told her. Ronald was like a spoiled child who had just been turned loose in a toy store. He had reverted to the seven-year-old boy who had a charge account with the candy store, the same boy neighborhood people on Fort Hamilton Parkway in Brooklyn used to talk about. However this rich widow had spent her money in the past, things were going to change. Ronald Mazarolla was going to show her how to spend it. Ronald was still that spoiled child.

As Donna got up from bed and went into the bathroom, she asked, "Want more champagne, dear?"

"Yeah," he said. "This time, don't forget the ice in it." Ronald the wine expert liked ice in all of his drinks. While in the bathroom Donna crushed a sedative into Ronald's champagne, filled the glass halfway, and swirled the amber liquid to mix the powder. "Here dear, drink this down," she smiled.

"Where's the fucking ice?" the soon-to-be wealthy Mr. Personality demanded. As always, Donna smiled and complied. As he drank the bubbly down he began to relax. He closed his eyes with the warm feeling of success permeating him. In a year or two, he thought, she would have an accident. He had killed before; he could surely do it again.

Just as Ronald was dreaming about butlers, mansions, Roll Royces, and chauffeurs, he felt a suffocating feeling. He couldn't move his arms and he dreamed that he was tied to the bed. The sensation of a pillow being over his face felt so real. The weight on his body felt like Donna. He thought heard her say, "Are you sure you want a silver Jaguar?" This isn't a dream, he realized. "Mother!" he tried to scream.

The previous year a hunter on the Mogollon Rim in Arizona had come upon the remains of what appeared to be a man and a woman. The woman's belongings indicated she had been a waitress.

The fire in the house in Old Westbury had been tragic. The fire marshals were sure it had been arson. Because the four victims were all Israeli nationals, federal officials handled the case. Their conclusion was that it had been the work of an Al Qaeda cell thought to be in New York.

Dr. Gilbert Marcus's body had been found in the stable. It appeared that his neck had been broken by a fall from the hayloft. His stiff body was found one Sunday at noon. It had been there all night.

# THE POLITICIAN

Mazzera San Andrea is a mountain village in the northeast Sicily. Guiseppe Livoti's grandfather had a different last name when he fled there from the other side of the mountain. His relocation was done in haste to escape the wrath of the avenging Argenziano family.

John's grandfather was Phillipe Simone, who had once placed a pitchfork into the chest of Vito Argenziano. As an adolescent, Grandfather Simone had followed the unwritten code of Sicily by defending the honor of his widowed mother. Seeing his mother in the arms of Vito had been too much for him to bear. Philippe was taught at birth that he must always defend the honor of the women of his family.

After relocating in Mazzera San Andrea, Philippe took his mother's maiden name, Livoti. He married, raised seven children, and at the age of ninety, died. One of his sons, Gianni, like many of the inhabitants of Sicily in the late nineteenth century, migrated to "La Merica."

Gianni began working in New York by purchasing bags of lemons wholesale and selling them in the Irish bars on the Bowery. He was often humiliated by the abusive drunks, but he extracted a high price for the valued lemons. The tart fruit, relished for its flavor when added to tea, acted as a peace offering to the distressed wives of drunken men. The lemons, with all their bitterness, would serve to sweeten the verbal profanation they were sure to receive when they returned home. If the drunken Irishman was lucky, the lemon would serve to influence his wife into a procreative encounter.

Gianni learned that a valuable commodity could demand a

high price. He realized the value of lemons in Irish bars, and he used that lesson in choosing the merchandise he would sell in the future.

After successfully earning enough capital, Gianni purchased a pushcart and carried a full line of seasonal fruits and vegetables. The pushcart soon became a horse-drawn wagon. Gianni realized he could maximize his profits by cutting out the middleman and growing his own vegetables. To this end he leased some land on the eastern shore of Virginia. With assistance from cousins whom he imported from Mazzera San Andrea, he was also able to amass a real estate portfolio by purchasing tenements on the lower East Side of New York City. He fathered two sons and five daughters. The sons would go to law school and not have the dirty fingernails of cafones. As students in PS 21 on Elizabeth Street, located across the street from his tenement, his sons John and Joseph, who had been given American names, would be made to study every day and would later become successful in their new homeland.

Gianni's success did not come easy. When he first located his pushcart on the corner of Orchard and Houston Streets near his Elizabeth Street apartment, he was told he had to pay for "protection." He refused, and he awoke one morning to find his cart had been burned. He began his business again and was promptly visited by Tomaso the tailor, a neighborhood hoodlum named for his well fitting attire. This time Gianni asked to see the boss. The thug laughed so hard at the request that he failed to see Gianni's raised knife before it was plunged into his chest. The fellow pushcart vendors saw Gianni step over the wounded thug, expose his throat by pulling his head back by a fistful of hair, and calmly draw his knife across the man's throat. He then packed up his fruits and vegetables and wheeled his cart away, leaving the hapless bully to bleed to death. Witnesses related the story to family members, because Sicilians never tell the police anything. Non capito niente, pronounced nunga capita nenta, was their motto.

Gianni returned to his tenement at 232 Elizabeth Street. Women leaning on their windowsills, the kind who notice everything, thought it odd that Gianni had returned home so early. The sentries of Elizabeth Street soon saw him walk out of his building with his shotgun in hand. He headed to the corner of Spring Street and then turned west toward Broadway. Anyone following him would have seen him turn north on Mott Street and enter the lair of the dreaded Chalutze "the butcher." There was silence in the small restaurant as Gianni entered. He approached the table where Chalutze was seated and said, "Your desgrazia is dead, and I will pay you nothing."

Chalutze motioned for his "guest" to sit. "Tomaso was a cafone," he replied in a calm voice. "Lei scaltro, you are smart. We can be partners. I help you, you help me, one hand washes the other. Capisce, paison?"


The Milky Way, the Southern Cross and the Coalsack were clearly visible to the naked eye from the boat deck of the QE 2 on that calm evening near the equator. As John Love pointed to the heavens, he displayed a mastery of the stars to his Millennium World Cruise companions.

John had learned to read the stars as part of his officer training in the United States Marine Corps. He had served in Okinawa near the end of World War II and had been called in as a reservist for the war in Korea where he was awarded the Navy Cross. John was a colorful casino lawyer and a former New Jersey Democratic Party leader who had helped to bring gambling to Atlantic City. As a member of the

Committee to Revive Atlantic City, which was created to restore the decaying old resort town, John Love accepted praise from business groups for being the force behind the 1979 statewide referendum. He went on to become counsel for the big casinos moving east from Nevada. Joseph Love, his older brother and former New Jersey state senator, had once held up a judicial appointment until laws that would be friendly to the casino lobby were passed. Charges were brought against his brother John for influence-peddling, but after the investigation the charges were dropped for lack of witnesses willing to testify. There were then accusations that the investigating agency had been hand-picked by the casino lobby. The accusations went nowhere.

The Love brothers, both graduates of Fordham Law School, had learned about the use of power from their father, a successful businessman.

The year 2000 was a presidential election year, and wealthy but aging John Love had been told he would be the Democratic vice presidential candidate. Along with his maturity he was a good-looking war hero, and he could easily carry the northeast. With unlimited funds from his wealthy father and the casino industry, he was exactly what Vice President Al Gore's campaign staff needed. John Love was a perfect complement to the vice president in his bid for the presidency.

John Love felt as though he was on top of the world. After this world cruise he would begin the campaign which he felt would one day allow his son to run for the presidency. His life could not be better—and it became much worse when the QE 2 docked in Southampton, England. It was there that he greeted Democratic Party strategists from the United States who would be dining with him in the Queen's Grill.

It was the look on the face of President Clinton's consultant James Carville that gave it away. This meeting would not be a congratulatory one.

"It was my wife Mary's investigator who found it out," Carville said with his Louisiana drawl, referring to Mary Matalin, his Republican political consultant wife. "God damn, she was happy about how that boy Vito never gave up. Why didn't you tell us?" Carville queried. "Didn't you know, man?"

John's father's identity and his history with organized crime, from which John had been so carefully insulated all his life, had been uncovered. All that had been kept secret would now be made public. This was the greatest disaster of John Love's life.

The numbness began in John's chin as James Carville revealed how his wife Mary's investigator, Vito Argenziano, had discovered the name change, Gianni's secret financing, and his profiteering in the casino industry. Then the numbness began to travel down his shoulder. By the time Carville revealed the complete details of the organized crime network, John's left arm was feeling numb, too. He did not associate this physical discomfort with his heart until he felt the pain in his chest. By then it was too late.

The last vision John Livoti Love had while lying on the floor of the elegant Queen's Grill was of the radiant Swavorski chandelier on the ceiling. His last thought was that the name Vito Argenziano was familiar.

# THE TERRORIST

Carlos Rameriz Umberto Montoya was better known as CRUM to the CIA, DEA, ODCSINT, the Mossad, Interpol, and all of the intelligence agencies throughout the world. They were all in agreement that CRUM was a threat to humankind. It was believed that he controlled OPEC, the Colombian drug lords, Mafia dons, international terrorists, and the American Democratic Party. In addition, the ADA, AMA, ABA, UFT, PETA,COPE, the Trial Lawyers Association, and Handgun Control were said to be his front organizations.

Senior Montoya was first noticed when he openly influenced business groups into supporting the military coup that deposed President Joao Goulart of Brazil in 1964. He was thought to have control over Alan Greenspan, David Duke, Jane Fonda, Ralph Nader, Abu Nadal, and Hilary Clinton. General Castelo Blanco, who took control of Brazil's central government after the coup, was thought to be financed by Senior CRUM. Through a lobby called Brazil's Action Democrats (BAD), Senior CRUM continued to organize private companies, media groups, and wealthy individuals to institute authoritarian rule. He began to build a formidable international investment enterprise.

CRUM was unapologetic in his belief that freedom of the press was a threat to the economic well-being of the world's population. In addition, he believed that disarmament of civilians is necessary for authoritarian rule. This explains why he most feared men like Colonel Robert Brown,Richard Nicotra Hunter S. Thompson, and Charlton Heston.

In 1967 CRUM became president of the National Bank of Brazil, a position he held for eight years. During this time he wove a formidable network of connections which he later used as the director of South America Communications. He invested in online industries, industrial manufacturing, and financial service businesses. It was believed that he was the brains behind Time Warner, the Cunard Line, the International Banking Fund, the United Nations, and Disney.

In the 1960s CRUM was the financial force behind research in the fields of cybernetics and genetics. When a breakthrough in cell renewal was at hand, it was said that Senior Montoya used himself as a test subject. Intelligence agents indicated that the experiment was a success. CRUM claimed to be born into an upper class family in Rio, Brazil's capital at that time, which was in 1910. He also made claims that he was descended from Portuguese nobility who had arrived in Brazil in 1802. None of these claims could be disproved. The rumor persisted that he was a well known figure in the hierarchy of the Third Reich.

The Bean Sprout Cafe in the Whitaker community of Eugene, Oregon, had to shut its doors forever. It was once a colorful restaurant that served Mediterranean-style pasta, seafood, and tasty vegetarian dishes. It should have been a success in the community with its old pickup trucks, cottages built during the depression, food coops, and cheap taverns that nourished the neighborhood.

The owner could not understand why he was the target of anarchists. At fifty-two years of age he considered himself a hippie, too. The anarchists broke windows and sprayed graffiti on the restaurant proclaiming "Yuppie gentrifying scum." There were numerous incidents of flattened tires on the BMWs and Saabs parked in the restaurant's parking lot. After a "Closed for good" sign was hung inside the door, the anarchists spray-painted the side of the building with "We Won!"

The leader of the AARP, the Anarchist Association and Resistance of the People, was said to be a former witch in her early fifties. The group started a grass roots school with subjects such as vegan cooking, compost gardening, yoga, and bomb manufacturing. Issues such as saving downtown trees, the logging of national forests, and animal rights were what galvanized their group. Teenagers dressed in black listening to punk rock joined with aging hippies looking like Peter, Paul, and Mary. The scene was described as "ecstasy meets marijuana."

The spate of anarchist activity had included vandalizing the sheriff's home and spray-painting the word "pig" on it. There were damaging attacks against computer stores, banks, restaurants, and Nike outlet stores. The graffiti slogans "Viva la Unabomber" and "Actualize Industrial Collapse" were seen everywhere in Eugene. A huge window on a downtown furniture store was smashed on one occasion when a sale on leather furniture was being advertised.

"I am not going to allow a group of urban terrorists to make our city streets a place where people feel unsafe," said Mayor Joe Cory after a member of Defender of the Downtown Trees vomited on him at a city council meeting.

The anarchists responded by saying that extreme times—high school shootings, corporate exploitation of Third World labor, destruction of native forests, genetic engineering of food—call for extreme measures.

At fifty-one, Wanda "the Witch" Wennerman was suffering from depression. Her attempts at becoming pregnant had been unsuccessful for the past four years. She had gotten the idea when she had read about Jane Seymour and Annette Benning becoming pregnant and bearing children in middle age. She was enthused that these celebrities had used their own eggs. A donor egg would not do for her. She wanted her child to have her own family's genetic makeup. She wanted the hair and eye color, height, and the talent in music and art that abounded in her family.

Wanda was met with one disappointment after another. Her eggs, fertilized with sperm carefully selected from a reputable sperm bank, never became implanted in her uterus. The American Infertility Association explained to her, "A woman is born with a finite number of eggs, and the genetic quality and viability of those eggs will diminish as you age. The natural reduction of ova and follicles will continue until the ovaries are depleted, somewhere around the age of fifty."

Wanda wished she could rewind her biological clock. Hoping it would allow her to find what her life was lacking, she quit "Jews for Jesus" and joined a Wiccan group. It didn't help. Her angst demanded revenge. Soon she was leading an anarchist group.

All Wanda really wanted was a baby, but she realized it was too late. She hoped bad sperm was the cause of her failure.

After she was released from being hospitalized for depression, her parents, who were members of the corporate structure she worked to tear down, insisted that she take a cruise to settle her mind. "Maybe you will meet a nice widower," her mother Sadie Wennerman, a major shareholder in IBM, told her.

Wanda the Witch sat astern on the boat deck staring at the ship's endless wake setting off continuous waves that would travel until they struck shore or another ship. What an interesting concept, she thought of the waves. They never die.

It was then that Wanda became aware of the distinguished gentleman in a Pierre Cardin jogging suit sitting on the deck chair beside her. His deep blue eyes cast a warm glow which she thought looked vaguely familiar. His appearance, with his white hair and neatly trimmed white beard gave her the impression that he was a kind, warm-hearted gentleman who had just entered retirement. They began to talk about the albatross following the ship and Shakespeare's The Rime of the Ancient Mariner. They continued their discussion of seabirds and the ecological fragility of the marine life in the ocean, then shifted their discussion to world events. Wanda told him about her antiestablishment activity in Oregon and her success in closing down the Bean Sprout Cafe. He smiled warmly as if he was remembering his youth. She took his smile as approval. Wanda loved this gentleman; he seemed so much like her. She shared with him the fact that she was a practitioner of witchcraft. Again the handsome gentleman smiled. When she told him of her activity as a member of Jews for Jesus, he said, "At one time I would have said that is a step in the right direction, but now I have learned to use tolerance and compassion to achieve my ends." He looked a bit older than Wanda, and she began to wonder about the viability of his sperm.

As Wanda walked back to her cabin on deck 4 she passed through the Royal Promenade, a collection of upscale shops like those on New York's fashionable Fifth Avenue and Paris's Champs Elyseés. Wanda passed Dusk, the QE 2 ladies' fashion shop featuring the Frank Usher collection of formal wear. She then noted that the perfume shop featured Vivienne Westwood boudoir fragrances. In the past she would have associated these shops with thoughts of bombs, fire, graffiti, and destruction. She stopped for a while and cast her gaze on the collection of children's stuffed animals in Harrod's window. She felt so at peace, and wondered whether the calming conversation with the mild-mannered gentleman had anything to do with this tranquil feeling.

Wanda was just settling in her cabin, planning a nap before high tea at four o'clock, when a knock came at the door. A serious-looking man with a British accent asked if he could have a word with her. The next day, in the same deck chair on the boat deck, Wanda waited for the warm, friendly gentleman. He arrived with a smile, his twinkling blue eyes and white hair contrasting against his smooth, tan skin. Again Wanda filled her early afternoon with pleasant conversation. She asked what the gold medallion around his neck with the words "Immer Da" stood for.

"It means 'Always There,'" he said after clutching it in his fist for a few moments. At this point she noticed that he spoke a little more quietly, as if reflecting on thoughts from another time. "Her name was Eva. My dog was Blonde."

Noticing tears in his eyes, she asked, "Who are you?"

"I am Carlos Montoya," he responded.

"No, I mean who, really, are you?" she pleaded.

"I am from Brazil. I was born in Rio in 1909."

"Why, then, have you got a German accent, and why have I been questioned about you by government agents from Britain's MI6, America's CIA, Germany's GSG9, and Interpol just for talking to you?" she exclaimed.

"They are probably agents in training, the good ones you never see," he replied. With a wink and a smile he asked, "Did you think they were after you for saving trees?" Mr. Montoya continued, "When you are young you do foolish things, and as you age you learn from your mistakes. Only with compromise have I learned to succeed." He paused. "I will tell you a big secret. I was really born on 20 April 1889. I am one hundred and fourteen years old. This is true. Ya."

"Stop it," Wanda laughed. "You don't look much older than I do."

"This I owe to the miracles of modern science. In the late sixties I used experimental drugs to reverse aging," he whispered. "I own a biotechnological company."

"Yeah, and I dropped LSD," Wanda chuckled. "Maybe that is why I cannot get pregnant. I have tried so hard."

"We are alike. You see, I could never get anyone pregnant," he said with a smile. "Maybe someday soon my biotechnologists can help us. They are near a breakthrough," he said with a serious look.

The ship was supposed to leave Durban, South Africa, on 27 March 2000 at 6:00PM. Wanda was on the deck watching the dockside activity when, at 6:40PM, she saw a Mercedes limousine arrive. A familiar figure exited the vehicle and hurried up the gangway. The QE 2 sounded two blasts and the graceful ship was immediately free from the berth. She thought that odd. She had been told that the ship never waited for anyone.

The next day, in her lounge chair, she failed to see her friend Senior Montoya. She waited there until evening. The seas were beginning to get rough as they entered the waters around the horn of Africa. It was then that she thought she heard an explosion. The sound came from below deck. She knew something was amiss when a lifeboat drill sounded. She had been on the ship for nearly three months and there had never been a drill at night before. The explanation was that there had been a freak explosion from a bottle of gin. Sadly, Mr. Montoya had been killed in his cabin, burned beyond recognition.

Are you kidding? Wanda thought. She knew about bombs—hell, she had taught classes in making them. It sounded like the standard cigarette/matchbook timer stuck to a champagne bottle filled with a combustible mixed with soap shavings. She really would miss that man. He had seemed so kind.

After docking in New York and waiting in line for a cab, Wanda was feeling sad about her lost friend when she noticed luggage with the initials "CRUM" on the side waiting to be picked up. A Mercedes limousine with darkened windows pulled to the curb and the chauffeur got out to retrieve the luggage. After he stowed the bags in the trunk the stocky driver approached her and gave her a small ice chest. With a Spanish accent he said, "Bring this to your gynecologist. He will know what to do. There are also pills and directions to follow."

"Wait, what is this all about?" At that moment she saw the rear window of the limo lower halfway and then quickly rise. For a brief instant she saw in the back seat a man with dark hair but with familiar blue eyes. The vehicle drove away, leaving her standing there holding a precious six-pack-sized ice chest with a Budweiser logo in the side.

Wanda felt her life had just changed.